I0746540
Spartan + FRIENDS

Hazel and Spartan's Big Show
Colouring and Literacy Book

Consolidating phonics knowledge with extended decodable text.

Word Count
Approx. 283 words

ow → **now, how, brown**
ai → **train, main, paid, again, wait**
ee → **see, green, feet, between**
sh → **show, shimmer, shine, brushed, she**
th → **with, their, the, them, both**
ch → **champion, cheerful, each, chosen, much**

High-Frequency Words
the, and, a, to, in, was, said, she, her, his, they, went,
then, when, their, had, with, for, as, out

Irregular Words
said, was, you, your, they, their, were, again, because, friend

Practice Words
Spartan, Hazel, show, arena, pattern, spin, slide, stop, ride, horse
practice, ribbon, judge, winner, crowd, cheer, proud, smile, brave

Teacher Prep Before Reading

Phonics Warm-Up: Review ar, an ow sounds using flashcards

Vocabulary Support: Introduce or discuss – arena, pattern,
spin, slide, ribbon, proud, judge, winner. Show short videos or
images of a reining pattern or sliding stop to build context.

Prediction Prompt: Ask: "What do you think Hazel will need to
remember before her big show?"

Hazel brushed Spartan till he shone like the night,
his coat sleek and glossy, his saddle fit just right.
The reining show loomed, the junior event,
she dreamed of the ribbons and hours well spent.

She studied the pattern, drew lines in the sand,
circles and rollbacks, all done as planned.
"Spins to the left, then a stop that slides,
i'll practice till perfect!" young Hazel decides.

Each morning, they trained in the crisp spring air,
Hazel sat tall with her plaited hair.
"Good boy, Spartan! You're learning so fast,
we'll nail those spins that make folks gasp!"

They trotted, they loped, they turned so neat,
dust danced softly beneath his feet.
Her boots felt snug, reins light in her hand,
together they moved like sea and sand.

The show day came with a bright sunrise,
banners flapped under open skies.
Fifteen riders lined up in a row,
each ready to shine in the junior show.

Hazel's heart thumped, she breathed in slow,
"Remember the pattern. Let your rhythm flow."
They warmed up steady, both calm and keen,
Spartan's black coat shimmered and gleamed.

In the warm-up pen, circles they spun,
each rollback sharper than the last one.
"Feel the slide," Miss Laura said, "Don't pull,
guide with your seat, stay calm and in control."

Then came the call: "Next, Hazel and Spartan!"
she whispered, "Stay calm, my brave-hearted partner."
Into the ring through the big white gate,
her pulse drummed loud, this must be fate.

The crowd grew quiet, the pattern began,
a spin, a stop, just as planned.
Hazel sat deep, gave a soft cue,
Spartan slid long, the crowd went "Woo!"

Each turn was tidy, each loop on track,
no stumble, no rush, no looking back.
A final salute, she patted his mane,
"Good boy, Spartan—you've done it again!"

Back at the gate, her friends all cheered,
Hazel grinned wide, the nerves disappeared.
When ribbons were handed, blue first, red next,
her name was called, she felt so blessed.

"Second place!" cried Hazel with pride,
she hugged her horse, love swelling inside.
"That was such fun, but no ribbon could measure,
the joy of this ride, and you, my treasure."

Activities (for after reading)

1. Re-read the story and circle words with ai sound (trail)

2. Find and <u>underline</u> all the words with ee sound (trees)

3. Write 3 new sentences that include ar sounds (farm)

____

____

____

____

____

____

____

4. Pretend to be Suki and act out how she might move.

5. Fill the gap: Pypah whispered, ___________ and slow

Activities (for after reading)

6.Write about your own "Big Show" it could be horse riding, dancing, football, or a talent show, describe what you practised, who came to watch, and how you felt before and after using lots of describing and feeling words.

____

____

____

____

____

____

____

____

____

____

Activities (for after reading)

7. Write some words that rhyme with "bee."

8. Can you name some things Pypah did to gain Suki's trust?

9. What do you think was the most exciting part for Pypah, being gifted Suki, or going on the trail ride? Why?

Activities (for after reading)

10. Can you retell the important parts of the story?

____

____

11. What was your favourite part of story?

____

____

____

12. Draw what Suki might be thinking in a thought bubble during their first lesson.

Activities (for after reading)

13. Draw a line back to the phonics sound that matches the word

ar sound	**or sound**	**sh sound**
horse	snort	she
start	brush	far
show	Spartan	short

14. Complete the words with the missing sounds:

Sp__tan
sh__
st__
cr__d
bru__

15. Colour in all of the story pages.

This is an example of a reining pattern:

Reining Pattern 6

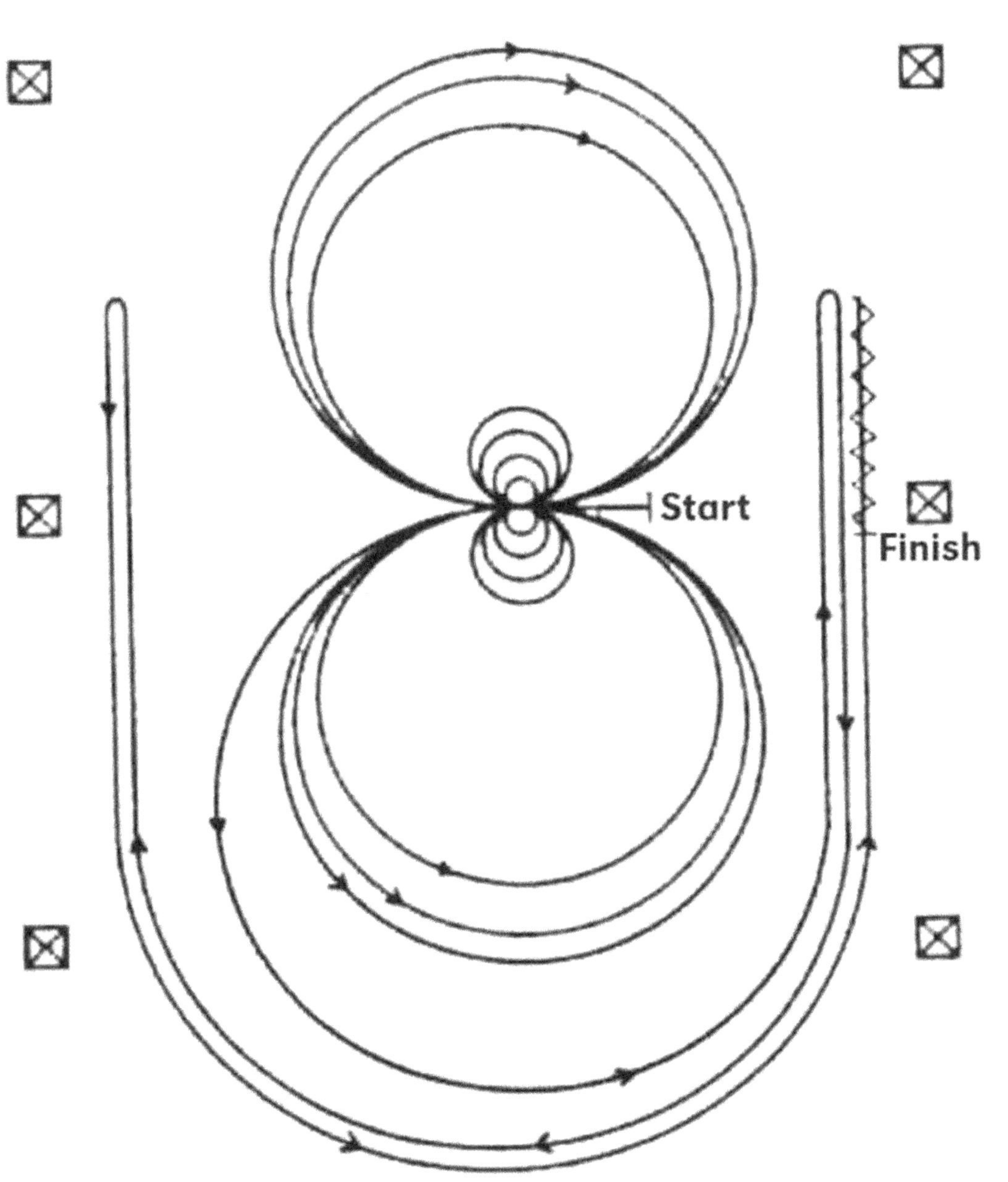

This is what the pattern means:

Horses may walk or trot to the center of arena. Horses must walk or stop prior to starting pattern. Beginning at the center of the arena facing the left wall or fence.

1. Complete four spins to the right. Hesitate.
2. Complete four spins to the left. Hesitate.
3. Beginning on the left lead, complete three circles to the left: the first two circles large and fast; the third circle small and slow. Change leads at the center of the arena.
4. Complete three circles to the right: the first two circles large and fast; the third circle small and slow. Change leads at the center of the arena.
5. Begin a large fast circle to the left but do not close this circle. Run up the right side of the arena past the center marker and do a right rollback at least twenty feet (six meters) from the wall or fence — no hesitation.
6. Continue back around previous circle but do not close this circle. Run up the left side of the arena past the center marker and do a left rollback at least twenty feet (six meters) from the wall or fence — no hesitation.
7. Continue back around previous circle but do not close this circle. Run up the right side of the arena past the center marker and do a sliding stop at least twenty feet (six meters) from the wall or fence. Back up at least ten feet (three meters). Hesitate to demonstrate the completion of the pattern.

Rider may dismount and drop bridle to the designated judge.

The patterns are to be worked as stated, not as drawn. The drawn pattern is just to give the general idea of what the pattern will look like in the arena.

Spartan + FRIENDS